FISHING
ON THIN ICE

BY ART COULSON · ILLUSTRATED BY JOHANNA TARKELA

STONE ARCH BOOKS
a capstone imprint

Published by Stone Arch Books, an imprint of Capstone.
1710 Roe Crest Drive
North Mankato, Minnesota 56003
capstonepub.com

Copyright © 2022 by Capstone. All rights reserved. No part of this publication may
be reproduced in whole or in part, or stored in a retrieval system, or transmitted in
any form or by any means, electronic, mechanical, photocopying, recording,
or otherwise, without written permission of the publisher.

Library of Congress Cataloging-in-Publication Data
Names: Coulson, Art, 1961– author. | Tarkela, Johanna, illustrator.
Title: Fishing on thin ice / by Art Coulson ; illustrated by Johanna Tarkela.
Description: North Mankato, Minnesota : Stone Arch Books, an imprint of Capstone,
[2022] | Series: Wilderness ridge | Audience: Ages 8–11. | Audience: Grades 4–6. |
Summary: As part of his thirteenth birthday, Jimmy Benge is spending a week
ice fishing with his friend, Ryan, in northern Minnesota at his family's lakeside
home. One day they get permission to go out further on the lake to try for northern
pike, and Jimmy catches a beauty—but a sudden snow squall turns the situation
dangerous. As the boys pack up to make their way back, Uncle Kenny's ATV flips
over and he is injured. It is up to the boys to get everybody home safely.
Identifiers: LCCN 2021030704 (print) | LCCN 2021030705 (ebook) |
ISBN 9781663974914 (hardcover) | ISBN 9781666329513 (paperback) |
ISBN 9781666329520 (pdf)
Subjects: LCSH: Cherokee boys—Juvenile fiction. | Ice fishing—Juvenile fiction. |
Storms—Juvenile fiction. | Survival—Juvenile fiction. | Uncles—Juvenile fiction. |
Minnesota—Juvenile fiction. | CYAC: Cherokee Indians—Fiction. | Indians of North
America—Minnesota—Fiction. | Ice fishing—Fiction. | Fishing—Fiction. | Survival—
Fiction. | Uncles—Fiction. | Minnesota—Fiction.
Classification: LCC PZ7.1.R63959 Fi 2022 (print) | LCC PZ7.1.R63959 (ebook) |
DDC 813.6 [Fic]—dc23
LC record available at https://lccn.loc.gov/2021030704
LC ebook record available at https://lccn.loc.gov/2021030705

Editorial Credits
Editor: Alison Deering; Designer: Sarah Bennett; Production Specialist: Katy LaVigne

Design Elements: Shutterstock/Mikhail Zyablov, Shutterstock/SvartKat

All internet sites appearing in back matter were available and accurate when
this book was sent to press.

Printed and bound in the USA. 4608

Table of Contents

CHAPTER ONE

Best Birthday Ever

"Where is he?" I asked, peering out the window. It was the night before winter break, and I couldn't wait for my best friend, Ryan, to arrive.

Winter break was the absolute best time of the year in northern Minnesota. The week was filled with all my favorite activities: snowmobiling, skiing, and ice fishing.

And the fact that it usually fell right around my birthday didn't hurt.

This year, I was turning the big one-three— I'd finally be a teenager! Uncle Kenny and Aunt Sammi had a special week planned for me. As part of the celebration, Ryan's parents had agreed to let him spend most of the week with me fishing out on our lake.

I always thought of it as "our lake," but really we shared Mudcat Lake with lots of other people. There were close to thirty homes and cabins spread out around the perimeter.

Aunt Sammi, Uncle Kenny, and I lived in a cabin on the east side of the lake. Though we were only about a fifteen-minute drive from my school and Uncle Kenny's clinic in Bemidji, it felt remote. We were surrounded by forests, lakes, and streams. If you asked me, it was the most beautiful place on Earth.

"I'm sure Ryan will be here soon, Jimmy," Aunt Sammi replied from the kitchen. She was working on my favorite dinner—fried walleye sandwiches and sweet potato fries.

I had lived with my aunt and uncle since I was a baby. We'd moved to northern Minnesota from our hometown in Oklahoma about four years ago. Uncle Kenny worked as a registered nurse, and the Indian Health Service had transferred him to a new clinic.

Just then I saw headlights coming up our driveway, illuminating the steady snowfall as a car approached our cabin.

"He's here!" I shouted.

"What's up, Jimmy?" Ryan said as he grabbed his duffel bag out of the car. His dad waved to my aunt and uncle.

"We're going to have so much fun this week," I said. I led Ryan through the attached garage and into the kitchen. "Let's throw your junk in my room. Walleye for dinner!"

"Yes!" Ryan said. "I'm starving!"

After dinner, Ryan and I went out to the garage. We needed to start gathering our gear for tomorrow's ice fishing adventure. Uncle Kenny had to work at the clinic in the morning, and Aunt Sammi was on a deadline for her next book. She was a writer and *always* seemed to be on deadline.

That meant Ryan and I would be going ice fishing by ourselves. We had both been out on the ice plenty of times before. But it would be our first time without my aunt and uncle.

Teenager at last! I thought happily.

A few minutes later, Uncle Kenny poked his head into the garage.

"Help yourself to any of the tackle in my big box on the workbench," he said, pointing toward the back of the garage with his lips. "I'll help you get my auger down as soon as I finish drying the dishes. I hang it up high so no one gets cut on the sharp blades."

"You boys remember to stay close to shore tomorrow—just fish in our cove where I can see you," Aunt Sammi added, peeking over Uncle Kenny's shoulder. "And keep an eye

on the weather. You know how quickly it can change this time of year."

"And please use your cell phone to call Aunt Sammi every couple of hours to check in, okay?" Uncle Kenny added. "Just to let her know you're all right."

Ryan and I nodded, but we were both focused on putting together our gear. Each of us filled a five-gallon plastic bucket with leaders, hooks, plastic lures, and other tackle. The buckets would do double duty, carrying our tackle out to the ice and then serving as seats when we flipped them upside down.

We each grabbed an ice-rod-and-reel combo from the rack over the workbench. Ice fishing combos were just over two feet long—a lot shorter than the rods and reels used in summer.

The combos were also very flexible. That allowed a fisherman or woman to feel every nibble.

"Boys," Aunt Sammi said, still watching us through the doorway, "you are listening, right? It can be very dangerous out there if you don't follow the rules. Safety is the most important thing on the ice. You always have to be thinking about it."

"Yes, ma'am," Ryan said.

I nodded and smiled in Aunt Sammi's direction. "Uh-huh, we hear you." Man, she was draining the fun right out of this birthday celebration.

"Now who wants some cake and ice cream?" Aunt Sammi asked.

Ryan and I exchanged grins. Just like that, my birthday was saved.

CHAPTER TWO

Watch Your Step!

I shook Ryan awake before the sun was up. He was a heavy sleeper and had been snoring most of the night.

"C'mon, buddy, time to catch some fish," I said, poking him in the ribs.

"Umph, don't—that tickles," Ryan grumbled. He sat up on the air mattress that took up half of my bedroom floor.

We threw on our jeans and sweatshirts and each pulled on a pair of heavy wool socks. It felt early, but by the time we made it to the kitchen, Aunt Sammi and Uncle Kenny were already there.

"Ready for your big day?" Uncle Kenny asked, sipping his coffee. He was dressed for work in his blue scrubs.

"Yes, sir!" Ryan said excitedly.

Aunt Sammi came over and kissed me on top of my head. "I'm going back to bed for a bit. Don't forget to call me in a couple of hours while you're out there fishing. And good luck! Catch us some fish for dinner."

Ryan and I each swallowed a donut and a glass of milk, then headed out to the garage. We put our five-gallon buckets in a short plastic sled. Then we added Uncle Kenny's auger and an ice scoop to the pile.

Finally we were off!

We dragged the sled about a hundred yards out into the cove behind our cabin. It was slow going considering both Ryan and I were bundled up like Arctic explorers. The temperature outside was just below zero.

We could see people fishing already up and down the lake. Several had pop-up ice shelters. Others sat on their plastic buckets, flipped upside down on the ice.

Ryan and I used the hand auger to drill a couple of holes about six feet apart. I used the scoop to clear the slush and ice chunks from the hole.

"It's frozen a good eight inches deep here," Ryan said, looking at his hole. "Plenty safe."

"Yeah, but you can't assume that the whole lake is the same," I reminded him.

I put a glow-in-the-dark tungsten jig on my line. I threaded a small pink plastic lure that looked kind of like a shrimp onto the hook.

"There could be some thin spots anywhere, especially close to shore or up at the top of the lake where the creek flows in," I added. "We'll have to be sure to check the depth if we decide to move."

Ryan lowered his baited jig into his hole and plopped down on his bucket. "Man, it's cold out here," he said, shivering and stomping his boots.

"Yeah, but there's nowhere else I'd rather be," I said, smiling at my buddy. "Ice fishing on my favorite lake with my best friend."

Just then, Ryan's pole jerked. "Got one!" he said. He reeled in a four-inch perch. "Aww, too small to keep. I've pulled way bigger out of this lake. Better toss this one back."

He gently removed the hook and lowered the fish back into his hole.

"Don't worry, there's more where that came from," I said.

As if on cue, my rod bent down toward my hole. I pulled up firmly and hooked the fish. I reeled and fought with it a bit.

Finally, I managed to drag an eight-inch olive-colored fish through the hole. Its belly

was dark orange, and its head had a bluish tint. A large black spot sat about where its ears would be. It was beautiful.

"Nice bluegill," Ryan said.

I pulled the hook from the fish's mouth and tossed it onto the ice. There were no size limits on bluegills, and this one was definitely big enough to eat. It was a keeper.

We fished for several more hours and even remembered to call Aunt Sammi to check in. I caught several smaller perch, and Ryan caught a sunfish and a bluegill but both were pretty little. None were keepers.

When the fish stopped biting, I used the auger to drill a couple of new holes a few yards from where we'd been fishing. I figured some of the bigger fish might be hanging around the weedline where the water got a bit deeper.

"You keep fishing," I told Ryan. "I'm going to walk around a minute to try to warm up."

I wandered back toward our cabin. I was glad I'd worn my insulated bibs. I was pretty toasty when the air was calm. Still, when the wind blew, it was biting.

I turned and headed back toward Ryan. As I got close, a bald eagle drifted by overhead. My family was Cherokee, and the eagle was a special bird to our tribe. It was special to Ryan's tribe too—he was Ojibwe, from the Leech Lake Reservation, just up the road from us.

Ryan saw me looking up and followed my eyes. When he saw the eagle, he turned back to me and nodded his head.

"That's a good sign," he said. "We're going to catch a ton of fish this week."

I gave Ryan a thumbs-up and walked a little farther toward shore. But then . . .

Crack! Splash! My right foot crashed through thin ice!

CHAPTER THREE

Give Me Shelter

Ryan dropped his rod and ran toward me.

"Stop!" I shouted, putting up my right hand. "I don't want you falling through the ice too."

Just then, more ice broke around me. My right leg went deeper into the water, soaking my pants up to the butt. I quickly flopped down on my belly, my left leg stretched out on the ice behind me.

Ryan dropped down onto his stomach too and crawled toward me. When he got close, he reached out his right hand, but he wasn't quite close enough.

He scooted slowly closer on the ice and reached out again. Our fingers barely touched.

"Hold on," Ryan said. "Almost there." He scooted another foot toward me.

"Here, grab on," he said. "I'll help you out. Stay on your belly, and we can both crawl back to thicker ice."

We made it safely back onto ice that would support our weight. I was okay, but my right pants leg, sock, and boot were soaked.

"Let's go back to the cabin," Ryan said. "It's too cold to stay out here with wet pants and boots."

I nodded, my teeth chattering. Ryan was right. That was enough ice fishing for one day.

* * *

"How was the fishing?" Uncle Kenny asked as he came in that evening. "Since I smell your aunt's world-famous wild-rice soup, I'm guessing not so great. Did you at least have a fun day out on the lake?"

"Well, I was on the lake," Ryan said. "Jimmy was *in* it."

I gave him a small shove. "Not funny, Ryan. Too soon."

Uncle Kenny looked at me. "Did you fall through the ice? Are you okay?"

I nodded. "I'm fine. Just punched through the ice with one foot."

"You know you have to be very careful out there—no ice is ever one-hundred percent safe," Uncle Kenny said.

"You're right," I agreed. "We were careful, and I *still* put my foot through the ice."

"Use the auger and tape measure wherever you plan to fish," Uncle Kenny continued. "You want at least three or four inches of ice to walk on. When we take the snowmobile out, I want five or six inches. At least eight inches when we're riding our ATVs on the ice."

Ryan and I helped set the table. The smell of Aunt Sammi's homemade bread made my stomach growl.

After we sat down and started shoveling food into our mouths, Aunt Sammi turned to Uncle Kenny.

"Ken, what do you think about the boys using your pop-up shelter tomorrow?" she asked. "I know you haven't gotten a chance to use it yet, but they were freezing out there today, even before Jimmy got wet."

"I don't see why not," Uncle Kenny said. "I'll show you boys how to use the portable heater. You'll be warm as a couple of baked potatoes in there."

Uncle Kenny refilled his soup bowl and grabbed more bread. "You boys might have better luck tomorrow with some live bait," he added. "What do you say we run into town after supper and grab some supplies?"

Ryan and I high-fived.

"That would be great," I said. "I have some birthday money I'd love to spend on new gear."

At the tackle shop, Uncle Kenny got us some wax worms and spikes, which fish seemed to love. I picked up a new ice combo, some more glow-in-the-dark jigs, and a few leaders.

When we got back home, Uncle Kenny took us out to the garage to show us his new shelter. It was like a big red-and-black tent with a flexible frame inside.

The shelter only took about a minute to set up, and was just as easy to take down. The sides and roof popped out, creating a shelter big enough to hold a couple of people and their gear. It also had a pair of zip-up doors on opposite corners and a small plastic window on each side to let in light—and to keep an eye on tip-ups.

Tip-ups were portable fishing devices. When the fish took the bait, the spinning reel under the tip-up would turn the flag guard on top, freeing the spring-loaded flag. That would be our signal to run out, lift the tip-up off the hole, and pull in the line by hand.

In Minnesota, each ice angler could have up to two lines in the water. Ryan and I both planned to jig in one hole inside with our rods, plus set a tip-up each in another hole outside.

"Thanks for letting us use your Christmas gift, Uncle Kenny," I said.

"Don't mention it, Chooch," he said, reaching down to ruffle my hair. "But you better catch us some fish tomorrow. I think we ate all the soup."

"You got it, Unk," I said.

CHAPTER FOUR

Setting Up Camp

The next day, Ryan and I dragged the shelter and some folding chairs onto the ice in the cove. Just like Uncle Kenny had shown us, we popped out the sides and roof of the shelter.

We drilled our holes and set our tip-ups before going into the shelter. Inside, we drilled our holes a few feet apart—that way we each had some elbow room for fishing. The portable heater, fueled by a small propane tank, kept us plenty warm.

Once everything was set, we baited our jigs and dropped them in our holes. Before I could say a word, my rod bent toward the hole.

"Yes!" I shouted. "Got one."

I reeled as quickly as I could, but whatever was on the other end was not making it easy. I pulled and fought, bringing it up inch by inch. Finally I managed to get the fish—a crappie—to the surface.

I held up my catch, admiring the fish. A pattern of blackish-green speckles covered most of its body.

It was the nicest fish I'd caught in the past two days—about a foot long. I unzipped the shelter door and tossed the crappie onto the ice near our sled. As I made my way back inside, I heard Ryan yelp.

"Fish on, buddy!" Ryan was reeling like mad. He pulled in a four-inch bluegill. He looked at the fish and frowned. "Aww, man."

"Catching a small fish and releasing it is better than not catching anything at all," I told him.

Ryan gently lowered the bluegill headfirst back into the water. "I guess," he said. "But I'd still like to catch something a little bigger. These panfish aren't much of a challenge."

"Yeah, I wish we could catch a northern or two," I said. Northern pike were one of the biggest predators in the lake. "Uncle Kenny and I caught a few last year, and they were real fighters. Uncle Kenny caught one that was more than forty inches long. And he released it! So it's still out there."

Just then my phone rang from somewhere deep in my parka. I grabbed at my coat and finally worked my phone out of my inner pocket.

"Hello?" I answered.

It was Uncle Kenny. "I'm taking half a day today, Chooch. I'll be heading home in a few minutes. You guys need anything from the store on my way?"

"Maybe some bigger fish," I joked. "The ones in this cove aren't much of a challenge. I know they're good to eat—just wish they put up a little more of a fight."

Uncle Kenny laughed. "I think I have just the thing. See you in a few." He hung up before I could ask him what he had in mind.

Ryan and I pulled in our lines and went out to haul in our tip-ups. We stowed the gear inside the shelter and zipped it up. It was lunchtime. Maybe the afternoon would give us better luck.

When we got to the house, Uncle Kenny was unpacking some bags. He put a big foam bucket on the floor and pulled off the lid. Dozens of small, gray fish swam and squirmed in the water.

"I grabbed some sucker minnows," he told us. "When you're fishing for northern pike, there's nothing like them." Then he tossed me a small, brown paper bag.

I reached in and pulled out a handful of smaller plastic bags, each with a leader and pair of hooks. Small, colored beads decorated the rigs.

"What're those?" Ryan asked.

"Quickset rigs," Uncle Kenny said. "They're great for catching northerns and muskies. You hook the live minnow with both hooks—I do one through the mouth and one farther back, just behind its dorsal fin. That way the minnow can still swim and attract the big fish."

I nodded. They were the same rigs I had used fishing for northerns with Uncle Kenny before. They seemed to work really well.

"I thought I'd take you boys out a bit farther after lunch and put out a few tip-ups where you might catch some northern," Uncle Kenny added. "What do you say?"

I looked at Ryan, then back to my uncle. "Is that really a question? Let's go!"

CHAPTER FIVE

Predator Becomes Prey

We went out on the ice and packed up the shelter and the rest of our gear. Then Uncle Kenny led us back up the hill to his shed. He brought out an ATV and Aunt Sammi's snowmobile.

"Go in and grab three helmets," he said. "You can drive the snowmobile, Jimmy. Ryan will ride with me. We'll drag the sled and gear behind us. Stay close and be safe. No monkeying around."

I nodded. I had gotten my safety certificate last year after taking a class at the armory. I could operate a snowmobile without an

adult now, but I was glad to have Uncle Kenny lead the way. I was still learning.

We rode out onto the lake and headed for the middle before turning north. I made sure to keep clear of other anglers and shelters as we flew across the ice.

After about ten minutes, Uncle Kenny slowed and came to a stop in an open expanse of ice. I pulled up beside him.

"This looks like a good spot," Uncle Kenny said, taking off his helmet. "Let's get your shelter set up and drill a couple of holes for the quickset rigs."

We set up our mini "fish camp" and put our chairs and the heater inside the pop-up shelter.

"I'm leaving the snowmobile here, but I do not want you driving it anywhere until I get back. Understood?" Uncle Kenny looked both of us squarely in the eye.

Ryan and I both nodded.

"Aren't you going to stay and fish?" I asked.

Uncle Kenny shook his head. "Aunt Sammi has some projects she wanted me to help her with back at the house this afternoon. Plus, you guys will have more fun without an old guy hanging around."

Ryan and I tied the quickset rig onto our thick, black tip-up line. The rigs included a metal leader that was almost two feet long. That kept the pike—with their razor-sharp teeth and powerful jaws—from biting through the line.

I reached into the cold water of the bait bucket and fished out a sucker. I handed it to Ryan, then grabbed another for my rig.

We both hooked them as Uncle Kenny had shown us and lowered the minnows into our holes. The minnows began to swim as we fed out a couple of feet of line.

I put my tip-up down over my hole and set the flag. We had barely gotten back into the shelter when Ryan shouted, "You've got one!"

Sure enough, my flag was up. I unzipped the door and dashed to my hole. Just then, Ryan's flag sprang up.

"You too!" I yelled. "Better get out here and pull it in."

Ryan was there in an instant. He pulled at his line, hand over hand. Pretty soon, we had both hauled in good-sized northerns.

"Think we should keep them?" Ryan asked.

In our fishing zone, we had to release any northerns that were between twenty-two and twenty-six inches long. My fish was about three feet long. Ryan's was just a little shorter.

Still, I shook my head. "There are bigger ones in here," I said. "Uncle Kenny said he wouldn't keep any under forty inches.

If we get one that big, I'm taking it to the taxidermy shop and getting it mounted."

"Yeah!" Ryan said. "That would look pretty tough on your bedroom wall."

We used pliers to carefully remove the hooks from the northerns' wide jaws and slid the fish back into the water. Then we put new suckers on our rigs before heading back to the shelter to finish drilling our holes.

While Ryan baited his jig, I fired up the portable heater. I looked out the window, but there were no flags up yet. I did see low, gray clouds—snow clouds from what I could tell— gathering off in the distance.

At least it's still pretty sunny here, I thought. *No reason to stop fishing.*

I tied a treble hook to my line and fished out a smaller sucker. I hooked it through the back, avoiding its spine. I lowered it into my hole.

I was just settling in my chair when Ryan gave a yelp of surprise. Whatever had hit his line had almost snatched his rod right out of his hands. He reeled in a really nice perch, close to a foot long.

"Keeper!" Ryan exclaimed. He dashed outside and put his fish in his five-gallon bucket.

My rod bent, and I gave it a small jerk. I reeled in a smallmouth bass of my own. Even though it was more than a foot long, I had to release it. It was illegal to keep bass in this part of the state during the winter.

Still, I was feeling good. "We're on a hot streak now," I said.

CHAPTER SIX

Hooking a Real Fighter

Ryan and I kept fishing for the rest of the afternoon. We each managed to pull in a few more fish—two perch, a bluegill, and three crappies. Ryan hauled in a good-sized crappie.

Eventually I pulled out my phone and set it into the mesh cup holder in the arm of my folding chair.

"How about some music?" I asked Ryan.

I opened my music app and scrolled down to a new playlist I had made. The phone started to play a thumping drumbeat.

"All right! Powwow music!" Ryan said.

A group of singers began to sing along with the beat of the drum.

"Not just any powwow music, ginalii," I said, calling Ryan "friend" in the Cherokee language. "Old-school stuff from Eyabay."

Ryan tapped his feet and nodded his head to the beat. "Great choice." He high-fived me just as his rod gave a big jerk. "Finally," he said. "I think this is a big one."

He was right—a big perch came through the hole. I reached in my coat pocket and pulled out the tape measure. "Let's see how long this one is."

"Fourteen inches!" Ryan said once I'd measured. "That's gotta be a record! Well, maybe not a record, but pretty big for a panfish anyway. It's no northern, but this will be better eating—fewer little bones."

When Ryan went out to put the fish in his bucket, I looked out the window and saw my tip-up flag had popped. I pulled in my line and hopped up. I went out the door just as Ryan was coming back in.

"Got one on my tip-up," I said, squeezing around him in the opening.

I raced over to my tip-up. The line was still going out, and the flag holder spun like mad. I picked up the tip-up and laid it on the ice next to the hole. Then I grabbed the line and began to pull it in.

The fish fought me, pulling the line out of my hand. I grabbed it again and pulled it hard, putting my whole body into it.

Ryan came running up. "That thing must be huge," he said. "Think it's a northern?"

"I think so," I said with a grunt. "Can't think what else might be out here that's this big and strong."

I fought the fish for what seemed like hours but was really only five or ten minutes. I had a good fifty yards of line on the ice when I finally got the fish to the hole. I could see its greenish body turning and struggling.

I pulled up firmly and got its head out of the hole. The minnow's tail stuck out of the northern's huge mouth. I wasn't sure the rest of the fish would fit through my six-inch hole—its body was as big around as my leg. But finally I managed to pull the fish all the way out and onto the ice.

"Holay!" Ryan said. "That fish has to be four feet long."

I took a couple of deep breaths. Then I pulled out my measuring tape.

"Would you measure him while I hold it here on the ice?" I asked.

Ryan ran the tape along the fish's length. He whistled. "Wow! Forty-four inches! You're keeping it, right?"

"You bet!" I answered.

I picked up the tip-up and carried it and the fish over to the sled to lay it out flat. Uncle Kenny had told me to do my best to keep the fish flat and undamaged. The taxidermist would need a good specimen to work with. Then I took its picture—the taxidermist would use that to get the colors just right on the mount.

I went back to my hole, baited the rig, and lowered it into the lake. Then I set the tip-up back in place.

"Let's go back in the shelter," I said to Ryan. "I'm starving."

We kept an eye on our flags and set our rods into small metal holders in the shelter as we snacked. Uncle Kenny had thrown in some venison jerky and a jar of his green tomato relish to go along with our roast beef sandwiches.

Ryan reeled in a small bluegill while he ate. He released it without missing a bite.

I changed out my treble hook for a glowing jig baited with a couple of spikes. Right away, I hooked a ten-inch crappie. It was the second good-sized crappie I had caught on a little baited jig.

I was surprised because I knew crappies really liked bigger food, like minnows. But I wasn't going to argue with my good luck.

"Nice one," Ryan said as he gave his line a tug and started reeling. "Give me a second, and I'll have one to add to the bucket too."

He was right. He held up a big bluegill, about eight inches long. "Let's throw these guys in the bucket."

Ryan headed out to add it to his bucket, but when he unzipped the door, we were in for a big surprise. It was snowing—hard.

A sudden squall had blown in over the lake. We could barely see the shore.

CHAPTER SEVEN

A Sudden Storm

The wind was blowing so hard, the door blew right back in Ryan's face. A cold wind carried snow into our shelter.

"Oh, man," I said. I stood up and joined Ryan at the entrance to the shelter. I looked out toward our tip-ups, but I couldn't see them through the heavy snowfall.

"Let's grab the tip-ups," I said. "We couldn't see the flags even if we caught something."

We put the fish in the bucket with the others and fought our way through the wind toward the tip-ups. We reeled them in and brought them back to the sled.

Then we stepped back into the warm shelter just as my phone rang. It was Aunt Sammi—sounding worried.

"Are you boys keeping an eye on the weather?" she asked. "The radar shows a big storm sitting right over us."

I nodded, even though she couldn't see me. "Yeah, we just looked outside. We're safe here in the shelter. Don't worry."

"Uncle Kenny is getting ready to head out to get you," she said. "You boys pack your gear and head back this way on the snowmobile if you feel safe enough to do so. Uncle Kenny will head your way on the ATV and guide you the rest of the way home."

"We'll be packed up and on our way back in five or ten minutes," I replied.

"Be careful, Jimmy," Aunt Sammi added. "It's really easy to get lost in a storm like this."

I hung up. Ryan and I quickly gathered and packed our gear quickly. He pulled up the stakes and helped me collapse the shelter. It almost blew out of our hands, but we were able to get it tied up and into the sled.

I checked the rope that connected the sled to the snowmobile, then climbed on. Ryan handed me my helmet, and we set out down the lake. We picked our way along slowly—I didn't want to hit anyone or anything.

"Man, I haven't seen a storm this bad in a long time!" Ryan shouted to be heard over the wind and snowmobile engine.

"I know!" I shouted back. I was a little scared. I'd never ridden through weather this bad before. "I hope we make it home okay."

At that moment, a huge ice shelter came into view just in front of us.

I let up on the throttle, but we kept sliding toward the shelter. My heart jumped up into

my throat as I swerved hard to my left and punched the throttle.

Ryan let out a shout as he almost flew off the snowmobile. He gripped me tighter, holding on with all his strength.

"That was a close one!" Ryan hollered.

I braked to a stop and gripped the handlebars tighter. Catching my breath, I looked back over my shoulder.

"Yeah it was," I said. "But we're going to make it home safely. I promise. Uncle Kenny will meet us just a little bit farther down the lake. Then we'll be home free."

"I hope you're right," Ryan said.

So do I, I thought. *So do I.*

CHAPTER EIGHT

Risky Rescue

I could barely see three feet in front of us, even with the snowmobile's headlight on. It lit the snowflakes like small, bright stars coming at the windshield of a spaceship. It was hypnotizing.

On the seat behind me, Ryan helped me navigate. "Let's steer closer to the shore," he said. "It'll be easier to follow the shoreline and stay on course."

"Good idea," I agreed. I adjusted our course, heading toward the lake's edge off to our left. "I bet Uncle Kenny will be doing the same. Keep a sharp eye out for his headlight."

We drove slowly through the snow. Keeping the snowmobile pointed in the right direction was exhausting. My shoulders were tense, and my arms ached. It was so hard to see through the driving snow.

I was also worried about thinner ice closer to shore, especially after my unexpected dip the day before. But we had to take a chance. If we went farther out on the ice, we might miss Uncle Kenny. Or worse—get turned around or lost in the blinding storm.

Then, off in the distance, I heard the rumble of an engine. It had to be Uncle Kenny's ATV.

Ryan must have heard it too. His hands tightened their hold on my shoulders, and he let out a loud whoop.

"We're saved!" he shouted over the storm.

"Not yet!" I shouted back. "We still have to find him."

I headed toward the sound of the engine, which grew louder. Finally, I spotted a small point of light way off in the distance. It was almost invisible through the snow.

"It looks like he's riding on the banks of the lake!" I shouted back over my shoulder. "He must have had the same idea we did."

We headed toward the approaching light. A dark shape—an ATV and rider—sped along the shoreline. We were about fifty yards away when I saw something that almost stopped my heart.

Bang!

The ATV crashed into a low obstacle near shore. I couldn't see what it was through the snow, but whatever it was was big enough to stop the ATV—hard.

The big ATV flipped end over end, throwing its rider into the air. Almost in slow motion, the rider flew out onto the ice, arms and legs flailing. The ATV landed heavily on all four wheels and bounced to a stop. Its rider lay very still.

"Uncle Kenny!" I shouted. "No!"

I sped up—thin ice or not—and raced toward the figure. As soon as our sled came to a stop, Ryan and I hopped off and hurried over.

Uncle Kenny, I thought frantically. He was lying so still on the ice. *Please be okay, please be okay, please be okay.*

As we approached, the man slowly stirred. He pushed himself up to a sitting position and flipped up his face shield. I let out a relieved breath at the sight of my uncle's unharmed face.

"Are you boys okay?" Uncle Kenny asked.

"Are *we* okay?" I asked. "We thought you were hurt—or worse! Are you all right? Can you stand?"

Uncle Kenny rubbed his left hip and leg. "I'm not sure," he said. "I landed pretty hard. I might have broken something. I don't know if I can get up. Maybe if you both give me a hand?"

Ryan and I reached down and grabbed Uncle Kenny under his arms. We gently lifted him up. Uncle Kenny put his weight on both of us and tried to walk but winced in pain.

"Help me get him to the snowmobile, Ryan," I said. "You drive, and Uncle Kenny can ride behind you. I'll drive his ATV and lead the way."

We helped Uncle Kenny onto the snowmobile. He groaned a few times and didn't say much. I hoped he wasn't going into shock.

I restarted the ATV and turned it back in the direction of our house. Ryan guided the snowmobile carefully behind me.

After about fifteen minutes of terrifying progress down the lake, I saw a small figure standing on the shoreline with a large, bright lantern. Aunt Sammi was lighting the rest of the way home.

When we pulled up, she hurried down to the shore. "What happened?" she asked. "Ken, are you hurt?"

Uncle Kenny winced. "I'm okay, just a little shaken up. I hit a stump near the shoreline and dumped the ATV. It was so hard to see in the storm. But luckily the boys were close and helped me home."

Together, we got Uncle Kenny into the house and onto the couch by the fire.

Aunt Sammi examined him from head to toe. "There's no swelling, and I don't see bones sticking out anywhere," she said. "But you're going to be really sore tomorrow. I was so worried for all of you. That's a bad storm out there."

She hugged Uncle Kenny tight. He cried out in pain. "Easy, hon. Squeeze me like that again, and you'll crack the ribs that the ice couldn't break."

We all laughed.

"Now that you're home safe, wanna see my fish?" I asked.

Uncle Kenny tossed a pillow at me. I guess he'd be okay after all.

CHAPTER NINE

Heroes' Reward

I could smell the bacon before I even realized I was awake. It was still dark out. Ryan snored away on his air mattress.

My stomach growled like a hungry wolf. I rubbed the sleep from my eyes. Then I smelled pancakes. My stomach growled again, even louder this time.

Ryan sat up. "What time is it?" he asked. "Is that bacon I smell?"

"I think it's time to get up and check on Uncle Kenny," I said.

"That was some adventure yesterday," Ryan said. "I thought the most exciting part of the day was going to be you hauling in a four-foot northern. But your uncle had to make it interesting."

"I'm just glad we were there to help him," I said. I pulled on my jeans and shrugged into my hoodie. "It could have been a whole lot worse if we hadn't been there."

"Howa!" Ryan said. It was an Ojibwe word that could mean everything from "all right!" or "okay" to "nice job!" It was sort of like our Cherokee word, "Hawa."

I nodded and smiled. We had been in the right place at the right time. And I was glad our fish story had a happy ending.

"Let's eat!" I said. "I smell bacon, and it's driving me crazy."

We walked out to the dining room. A delicious-looking spread of food covered the table. I saw bacon and eggs, pancakes and maple syrup—and my favorite, cheese grits.

When they saw us, Aunt Sammi and Uncle Kenny stood up and applauded. Ryan and I took a step back and stared at them.

"Wado, boys. Thank you," Uncle Kenny said. "I set out to save you yesterday, and syou ended up rescuing me."

"Our heroes," Aunt Sammi added. "Your uncle and I can't thank you both enough for your quick thinking yesterday. You got him—and yourselves—home safely in that storm. We figured a special breakfast would be a good reward."

I blushed, a little embarrassed by all of the attention. "I'm just glad we were close when you had your wreck," I said. "It was scary to watch—I can't imagine what it felt like to actually be *in* the accident."

Aunt Sammi's dark brown eyes started to tear up, and she wiped at them. "Sit down and eat while it's still hot," she said, reaching down to put a pancake on each of our plates.

"How are you feeling today, Uncle Kenny?" I asked.

"I'm bruised and sore but unbroken," my uncle said with a chuckle. He sat down and started to load his plate with cheese grits and a pile of bacon. He took a sip of coffee, then grinned at us, like he had a secret to share. "In fact, I took today off from work because there's something I have to do."

I looked at him and raised an eyebrow. "What?"

"I need to take my wife and my two favorite boys out ice fishing for northerns," he said. "We'll make a whole day of it."

"Really?" Ryan asked.

"Yes, but this time we're just going out to the middle of the lake right here." Uncle Kenny tilted his head and pointed his lips out past our cove. "I'm sure there are some big fish closer to home."

I took a bite of bacon and shoved a big chunk of pancake into my mouth. Maple syrup dripped down my chin.

"I bet you're right," I said, wiping my chin with my napkin. "Maybe Ryan and I can give you both some pointers. After yesterday, I feel like quite the expert fishing guide. I mean, I am a teenager now, after all."

Uncle Kenny chuckled and put a hand on my shoulder. "Yes, Chooch," he said. "You are a teenager now and growing up fast. I'm proud of you. I bet you could show us a thing or two."

I grinned and ate more pancakes. I'd had no idea that turning thirteen would be filled with so much adventure. But after yesterday's excitement, I was ready for whatever was coming my way.

About the Author

photo by Ivy Vainio

Art Coulson, Cherokee, was an award-winning journalist and the first executive director of the Wilma Mankiller Foundation in Oklahoma. He grew up fishing and crabbing most weekends with his family, especially his mother, who was an avid angler. These days, Art spends as much time as he can at his lake cabin, where he loves to ice fish for panfish and northern pike. He is the author of several books, including *The Creator's Game*, *Unstoppable*, and *The Reluctant Storyteller*, as well as the Wilderness Ridge titles *Lure of the Lake* and *Trophy Buck*. Art lives in Apple Valley, Minnesota.

About the Illustrator

photo by Johanna Tarkela

Johanna Tarkela is a digital artist who loves playing with strong, atmospheric light and shadow in her realistic-style work. Born and raised in Finland, she spent a lot of her childhood outdoors, surrounded by the beautiful Nordic nature, which is reflected in her favorite themes to draw. She has been drawing since she was a young child and has worked on many children's books. Johanna later attended university to study illustration in England, where she currently resides and works as a freelance illustrator, represented by Lemonade Illustration Agency.

Glossary

angler (ANG-glur)—a person who fishes for pleasure

auger (AW-guhr)—a tool that uses a large drill bit and blade to drill holes in the ice; an auger may be hand-operated or use a small electric or gasoline motor

certificate (ser-TIF-i-kit)—a paper showing that a person has met certain requirements

jig (JIG)—a lure that is jerked up and down while fishing; jigs usually look like insects

leader (LEE-duhr)—a length of thin metal wire used to attach a hook and bait to a line in order to keep fish from biting through the line

lure (LOOR)—a fake bait used in fishing

portable (POR-tuh-buhl)—easily carried or moved

reel (reel)—a spool or wheel on which fishing line is wound

reservation (rez-er-VAY-shuhn)—an area of land set aside by the U.S. government for Native Americans

taxidermist (TAK-si-dur-mist)—a person whose job it is to prepare, stuff, and mount the skin of animals

tip-up (tip-uhp)—a portable device used while ice fishing to suspend bait through a hole drilled in the ice; lets anglers see when a fish takes the bait even when they're not holding a rod

tungsten (TUHNG-stuhn)—a hard metal that is used to harden other metals, such as steel

Talk About It

1. Uncle Kenny and Aunt Sammi share several safety tips with Jimmy and Ryan before the boys go out on the ice by themselves. Based on those tips, what do you think are some of the dangers of ice fishing? How would you make sure that you were safe on the ice?

2. There are a lot of rules to learn about ice fishing, including size limits for different types of fish and seasons—when you are allowed to catch and keep different species. Why do you think there are so many different rules for different types of fish? Why might they be important?

3. Anglers have to learn new skills, including how to use different types of fishing and safety equipment. Have you ever started a new hobby like ice fishing or something else? What are some ways you learned new skills? How did you improve your skills?

Write About It

1. Jimmy loves winter break because it's close to his birthday, and he can spend time doing things like ice fishing. Write a paragraph about your favorite time of the year. Why is it special? What are your favorite things to do during that time?

2. What are some of the ways that anglers fish for different types of fish? Write a list of tips you learned from this story. Look back through the book if you need help or ideas.

3. Have you ever been ice fishing? Write about one of your favorite memories out on the ice. If you haven't been, imagine the perfect ice fishing trip. What made (or would make) that ice fishing trip memorable?

More About Ice Fishing

Ice fishing is a cold-weather activity that has been around for thousands of years. Today, anglers fish for food and fun through holes drilled in the ice that forms on lakes or rivers in the winter.

During the winter in many northern states, whole "cities" spring up on large frozen lakes. Many anglers fish simply, sitting on overturned plastic buckets and using short ice fishing rods. Some anglers, however, set up portable ice shelters or use elaborate fish houses. Fish houses can be heated and have bunk beds—some even have carpeting and a TV!

Before you step foot outside, dress warmly. Layers, including a warm hat and gloves, are essential to staying safe on the ice. A good pair of boots with detachable cleats or metal coils will help you keep your feet on the ice. A set of ice spikes, worn on a cord around your neck, can help you pull yourself out if you fall through thin ice.

You can start ice fishing with minimal equipment. All you really need—beyond a fishing rod—is an auger, chisel, or ice saw to make a hole in the ice.

As you spend more time on the ice, though, you might want other equipment to keep comfortable outside or improve your chances of catching fish.

- Tip-ups can be used to put additional lines in the water. Check your state's laws to make sure you don't have too many lines in at once. (Some cities also regulate the size of holes that can be drilled in the ice.)

- Portable ice shelters can keep you warmer outside and can hold one person, or many, depending on the size. Small propane heaters can also keep the shelters warm.

- A long metal or plastic ice scoop can help clear slush and ice chunks from a hole.

- A foldable chair or stool can be more comfortable than sitting on an overturned bucket all day.

- Battery-operated fish finders show the position of bait and any fish swimming under the ice.

- A small plastic sled is ideal for hauling equipment on and off the ice by hand. If you have access and adult supervision, you could also use a snowmobile or ATV.

Check Out All the
Wilderness Ridge Titles

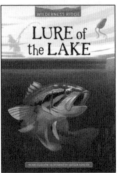